Zoric the Spaceman

written and illustrated
by PETER KINGSTON

*This story has been adapted
for easy reading
and details are given
on the back endpaper.*

First edition

© LADYBIRD BOOKS LTD MCMLXXXII

A New Home

Ladybird Books Loughborough

Zoric is a spaceman. One day he was
in his spaceship.

But something went wrong.
"Oh dear! What can I do?" he said.

Zoric looked at his map. "I will land
on this planet," he said.
It was Earth!

Soon Zoric came down from space.
He was over the trees.

"These trees look very big," he said.

Zoric landed his spaceship in the forest. It came down with a bump.

He got out and looked round.

"Oh dear! What big flowers!" he said.

Then he heard a noise and he hid under a flower.

A squirrel saw Zoric.
"Hello. You're very little," he said.

"No," said Zoric. "I'm not little.
You are very big." And they laughed.

Zoric said, "I must see
what's wrong with my spaceship."

Then Zoric looked very sad. "I cannot mend my spaceship. I cannot go home." He began to cry.

"Don't cry," said the squirrel. "You can live in the forest with us."

"Come with me," he said and he ran away.
"Wait for me!" said Zoric.

The squirrel came back. "Jump onto my back," he said. And off they went.

They jumped over a stream.

They ran through the trees.

Then they stopped
and Zoric saw an old teapot.

Zoric looked inside the teapot.
"Yes, this will make a good house."

"Please will you take me back to my
spaceship?" Zoric asked.
And off they went again.

Zoric got his space saw. When he pushed the red button it went **buzz**!

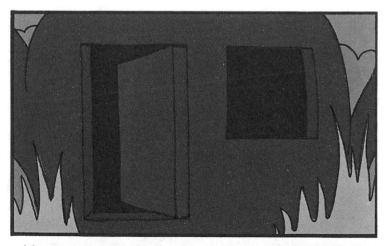

He went back to the teapot and with his saw he cut a door and a window in his house.

Then Zoric cleaned his new house.
He threw out leaves and twigs.

"I must go now," said the squirrel,
"but I'll come back soon."

Next, Zoric made a table and a chair.

Then he made a cupboard
out of a box.

With his saw he cut a tin
and made a bed.

Soon the squirrel came back.
"Come out, Zoric!" he said.

The squirrel had come back with some
friends. There was a grey mouse

and a big blackbird.
"Hello, Zoric," they said.

Zoric was very happy. He had a new, teapot house and some new friends.

Helping the Birds

When Zoric sat up in his bed one day,
he heard thunder.

He looked out of the window.
It was raining.

Zoric made his breakfast.

He was eating it when he heard
a noise at the door.

It was the blackbird. She was very wet.
''Please come, quickly!'' she said.

Zoric got dressed and ran after
the blackbird.

When they got there she said to him,
"Look! The branch is broken and
my baby birds have gone."

"Please can you help?"
said all Zoric's friends.

Zoric began to think.
"I know what I can do," he said.

"Please will you take me to my
spaceship, Squirrel?"

When they got there Zoric went inside his spaceship.

He got out a big box.

He put the box on his back.

The squirrel asked, ''What's that, Zoric?''

Then Zoric pushed one of the buttons.

He went up in the air. ''This is my space pack. Now I can fly,'' he said.

Zoric and the squirrel went back
to the blackbird.

"Please find my baby birds, quickly,"
she said.

Zoric pushed the button.
Up, up, up he went.

"I'll fly over the tree and look,"
said Zoric. Then he saw the birds.

They sat on a branch in the tree.
They couldn't fly and Zoric couldn't
get to them.

"I'll get you down, soon," he said
to the birds.

He went down to tell the blackbird.

Quickly he went to get the space saw from his house.

Soon Zoric was back up in the tree.
''I'll cut away the branches
with my saw.''

The baby birds were afraid.

Buzz! Buzz! went the saw.

Soon Zoric could get to the baby blackbirds. "Jump on!" he said. "Now we'll go down."

"Well done!" said the mouse.

"Hooray!" said the squirrel.

"Thank you, Zoric," said the
blackbird.

"That's all right," said Zoric.
"You are my friends."

Then the blackbird
looked at the branches.

"I know," she said, "let's take these
to your house. You can make a fire
with them."

"Oh yes!" said Zoric. "Then I shall
be warm in winter."

"I'll help you," said the little mouse.

Zoric cut the branches with his saw
and made a big pile of logs.

"I shall be warm this winter," he said,
and then he made a cup of tea.

Notes to parents and teachers

This series of books is designed for children who have begun to read and who need, and will enjoy, wider reading at a supplementary level.

The stories are based on Key Words up to *Level 5c* of the Ladybird Key Words Reading Scheme.

Extra words and words beyond that level are listed below.

Words which the child will meet at *Level 6* are listed separately, in case the parent or teacher wishes to give extra attention to these words and use this series as a bridge between reading levels.

Although based on Key Words, these books are ideal as supplementary reading material for use with any other reading scheme. The high picture content gives visual clues to words which may be unfamiliar and the consistent repetition of new words will give confidence to the reader.

Words used at Level 6

day	when	birds
very	door	box
round	next	fly
don't	friends	find
live	wet	
old	baby	